Beyond What is Normal

Printed in the United States of America

CourseyLands Publishing

First printing, 2019

ISBN 9781093662153

*for all my brothers and sisters
who faced and are facing persecution*

1

September 18, 1942

The warm sun was shining in my face, almost like it was smiling back when I grinned. I followed the stone path through the trees and to my neighborhood. It was warm, but there were still puddles on the ground, waiting to rise up into the sky again. I looked past some greenery, to see a wide open field with sheep and their shepherd. I heard birds chirping in the trees above me, and the smell of rain still sat in the air. I waved at the old shepherd; as I did everyday on my walk home. A ferrell dog ran past me and started to bark, when he spotted my neighbor's plump, grey cat. It was afternoon and I walked inside to find my parents sitting at the dining table, talking. I could tell it was serious, so I went upstairs.

It had been a beautiful day in Wisła, Poland, and I had spent my day attending the town's small school a few blocks from home, and walking through the busy market, buying food with my small amount of money. I walked upstairs and jumped when I unexpectedly saw my little brother spying on my parents, around the corner.

"I think they're talking about those German guys coming here," he whispered.

"I'm sure everything is okay Kacper, and don't eavesdrop. It's rude." I said, trying not to smile at his curiosity. "Oh, and they're called Nazis," I murmured as I closed my bedroom door. I stepped into my homely bedroom, full of books, posters, and lots of plants.

Sitting in front of my olive green vanity, I looked at a couple of family pictures. Then I looked out the window. What were Mother and Father talking about? Of course I knew the War was still occurring, but could the Nazis be coming here to persecute our religion?

My family had always been Jehovah's Witnesses since a man, years ago, came and taught few people about the Bible. My great grandparents were one of them.

I had heard of some persecution of Jehovah's Witnesses, but I never imagined our small town, Wisla, Poland, would even be known by the Germans. It had been three years since World War II broke out, and that is when my story began.

"Iza! Come down here please!" My Father called from downstairs.

I fled down the stairs, skipping a few as I went. "Yes?"

"Something has been going on around town that we need to talk about," Father sighed.

"Should I get Kacper?" I asked, pointing upstairs.

"No, it's alright." My mother quickly responded.

I sat down feeling worried.

"Iza, fathers have been being taken away from their families by the Nazis in the past few days," my father said.

"Families that we know? Witnesses?" I asked.

"Yes," Father exhaled, "Klara's father was taken away yesterday."

I thought of all the kind families we had been friends with all my life. I felt my eyes water, and my heart rate quickened.

"We'll have to be careful," Father said, turning his head to my mother; they held hands. No one mentioned it, but we all knew. Jehovah would help us through it, no matter what would happen. I decided to stay faithful and trust in my family.

I sprinkled some water onto my plants that sat so peacefully on the window sill.

The plants were peaceful because they didn't know. They didn't know about the things that happened around them. *I wish I had never even knew about the war*, I thought, *I'd rather just live a peaceful life. Without knowing, just like the plants.* I stopped. *No.* I needed to help. I was sixteen and my parents expected me to be strong.

"Are you okay?" Kacper asked. He had a worried voice.

"Oh, of course," I said, realizing I had been staring off for awhile.

Kacper smiled and skipped out of the room. He was always so happy. I guessed most children were like that, without many worries in the world, and not seeing differences in people by how they look. They have so much feeling, but not too much that it overwhelms them.

I took out my homework from school. Science was my favorite subject in school, and I loved learning about plants and medicine. I wanted to go into the health field, like a doctor or nurse, but mother and father said it takes college and a lot of work that would take me away from spending time with family, and studying the Bible. Until I started looking for a job, I decided to just focus on what was happening in the present, and not worry about the future too much. It was hard. The Nazis were starting to invade, and now were arresting Jehovah's Witnesses. How could I not be afraid?

2

September 18, 1942

The office was dark, musty, and only filled with suspicion. It was quiet most of the time, with only the sounds of rustling paperwork and the clicking of pens. Every half hour or so, a soldier would walk in, and every several hours, my father walked through the door.

I worked for my father at the secret office of Gestapo.

The Gestapo was a secret police group that thousands were involved in.
My father was a captain of a small group around fifteen soldiers that went around town stealing people, sending them to camps, or killing them. I worked for Father in the Gestapo office that was house in a small basement in a town called Wisla, Poland... My father and his fellow group leaders that also traveled to Poland from Germany, bought the

building. I had to come here with my father because I didn't have a mother that I could stay in Germany with, and my father needed a secretary to work for him. So that's what I did everyday, getting his mail, organizing, and other boring paperwork.

Although I would love to, I could not escape this terror of hearing about all the things they did every day, and watch victims get pulled away from their families. Every night I sobbed because I hated my job and I hated my father. If I did try to escape, my father would probably hit me or lock me in my room.

After Mother died from lung cancer when I was six, he was never the same man. He didn't show any emotion but anger and frustration. When my mother was alive she told me about this God who lived in the sky that I could pray to for help, but if there was a God, how could he let all this happen? Would he really listen if I tried to talk? I didn't believe in any of it, I couldn't.

I sat at my desk organizing papers, when my father walked into the office. I looked up and sat up straight. Smiling, I watched him walk over to my desk. Of course my smile wasn't real, but I tried everything I could to get him to smile. He rubbed his scratchy beard that needed to be shaved.

"Are you done with this stack?" He said with almost no emotion in his tone or face. He was, by far, the hardest person to read, and it was very frustrating.

"Yes, I just have to-" I began.

"No I don't want to hear what you have to do still, just do it," he said, closing his office door.

I sighed. Pinning back my long blond hair, I watched a scene in front of me that was much like all the other scenes I watched everyday, helplessly.

"Hey! What did I say?!" The man yelled, pulling his face closer, and closer, to a young soldier's face

"I'm sorry, I just-"

"No! I don't care if you're sorry!" He snapped.

"I'll do better," the soldier said, staring straight into the evil man's eyes, but the man just shoved him closer to the door.

I heard a door open, and a groan from behind me. It was my father. His eyebrows furrowed, and eyes widened.

"What is going on?!" He yelled.

The evil man looked at Father, "My apologies sir, the young one was disobeying," he said, standing up straight. He puffed out his chest with pride, but there really was nothing to be prideful about.

"Well I can deal with it!" My father sternly replied. "You are to take roll and do your paperwork, not shove my soldiers around!" Father yelled.

The man looked at his shoes and walked back to his desk. I tried not to giggle at the man who looked so disappointed, like a small child who was on time-out.

I don't think adults should be respected more than kids. The sayings like, "respect your elders," and "grey hair is a crown of beauty," are both very true. But why should kids be all thought of as unintelligent and rude, when adults' lives are often more messed up, so they become the rude ones?

My father didn't really respect either kids or adults. The only person he respected was Adolf Hitler. Hitler was the leader of all Nazis. He thought his destiny was to kill, and he hated Jews, Jehovah's Witnesses, and other religions and races. Hitler began World War II. I was raised to believe in him, but I didn't. I felt quite the opposite, I hated him. He was cruel and a terrible role model. Especially for my Father. He used that cruelty and anger towards his workers, guards, and soldiers. Everything was included in the mix of my Father's personality, my mother passing away, an unhappy life, and a role model, whose example was the worst you could think of. All those things made my dad who he was.

I sometimes enjoyed studying everyone's individual mixture of aspects in their life that made up who they were. It was hard, because all day every day, I was only surrounded by soldiers whose most personalities were dull and emotionless.

I hated when the young men were so disrespected like they were. They were far from their families and doing things that a lot of them probably didn't want to do. I couldn't do anything about it, so just watched from a distance.

3

September 18, 1942

I tried to focus on my homework, but it was so hard to keep my mind off Klara and her poor family, and all the families that were suffering from the war. I could tell my mother was having trouble keeping positive too, when I was watching her cook.

"I saw a good sale on some vegetables at the market today," I mentioned, trying to lighten the mood.

Mother perked up. "Is that so?" She smiled. "Sorry I'm in such a dull mood," she spoke, with a sigh.

"It's alright Mother, you don't have to put on a smile right now. I understand," I replied, walking over to the kitchen. I started to wash some dishes, and peel the potatoes.

Of course I felt plenty of fear, but there was definitely a fair share of contentment, and faith. I knew my family was strong, and I needed to keep that strength alive.

My thoughts were interrupted when there was a knock at the door. Mother and I looked at each other with worry. We had become more paranoid since the war started and every knock at the door seemed ominous.

My father came downstairs and signaled to stay in the kitchen while he answered the door. Mother and I stepped back. I held her arm tightly and said a silent prayer. The door opened, and I heard a voice. A voice that gave me comfort, love, and nostalgia. "Father!" My twenty year old sister, Lana, cheered. It felt like the whole world sighed with relief. I ran out the kitchen, towards her, and hugged her as tight as I could. Her husband walked through the door smiling, put their suitcases down, and hugged my parents. Lana squished my face and gave me another hug.

"I can't believe you're here!" I squealed.

"I missed you so much, Iza!" She said, with the biggest smile. Her smile was beautiful, and made my heart melt. I was so happy. She had left six months after the war started, to England. She started a new life, traveling with her husband to teach people about the Bible, all around the world. She met her husband there, and I had only met him once until now. I turned my head to him. His name was Walter; he was very kind and had a good sense of humor. I liked him. I was glad my sister married him because he was someone who actually enjoyed talking to people younger than himself, like me.

"Iza! It's great to see you again!" He exclaimed.

I smiled. "You too!" We hugged, and I was about to ask the both of them how the trip over was, when I heard, "Lana!" It was Kacper running down the stairs, almost tripping. He ran and jumped on Lana and she almost fell over, but caught her balance.

Mother served a delicious homemade meal made of chicken thighs & breasts, with peas, baked potatoes, and a sauce Mother made, but never told anyone what was in it.

Lana and Walter shared great experiences they had in the past year and a half in England. They seemed really happy there in England and I could tell Mother and Father were very proud of them. After we caught up on England, we explained what had been happening in the past few weeks, about the Nazis and how many of our brothers who share our religion had been taken away by the Nazis.

"We came to support you all. It's going to be alright," Lana reassured us. It was a tall order she was giving herself, but she had so much confidence and love, that it seemed nothing could stop her. I always looked up to my sister ever since I understood her presence as a very small child.

She was one of the most caring people I knew, and it had been hard for me without her. When we were kids, we would take turns telling each other things that interested us. She would usually talk about how she dressed her doll that day, and I would always go on and on about facts from a science book, how much my plant had grown in the past week, and different medicines that I would use when I became a doctor.

She wasn't interested, but she listened, asked questions, and wouldn't interrupt me. I try to be that way with Kacper. It was hard.

"I was thinking about what we could do to help the brothers in prison, "Lana said with a grin.

"All we can do is pray for them, darling," Mother said disappointedly.

"No, we can do more. I did pray and think about it, a lot," Lana said. "And I have a plan."

Mother and Father glanced at each other, and Lana explained what she wanted to do.

"All those prisoners really need is God's help," she began. "I'm sure they pray so hard everyday, and that's great. But they can have more. We can give them Watchtowers when we send in our monthly food contribution!"

Watchtowers were magazines that the headquarters of our religion produced, to encourage people with Bible truths.

"Lana dear," Mother said while holding on to Lana's hand from across the table. "We can't risk getting caught."

"Why not?" Lana asked ambitiously. "We should do anything to help the brothers! They're suffering, and Jehovah will make sure we'll be okay!" She exclaimed with no doubt.

Father sighed, and Walter put his arm around Lana, resting his hand on her left shoulder. "I'll do it." Lana said looking down so she wouldn't see anyone discouraging the idea. "I want to make Jehovah proud." She smiled, and got up to put their luggage upstairs.

"How do you feel about it, Walter?" I asked.

"Well," he looked down. "I don't want to lose her." He looked up, and grinned. "But I am incredibly proud of her, and she's the strongest person I know," he said confidently. You could tell he was truly in love with her.

"The... lovely garden, made me..very happy," Kacper pronounced from his book. "I think I'm getting better!" He said cheerfully, looking up at me. His dark brown eyes glistening.

"You sure are," I replied, messing up his wavy brown hair. He was behind in reading, but was determined to get better, and I was determined to help him. After he finished reading aloud his short, easy, storybook, I read him the fifth chapter of "Black Beauty." An American novel that our aunt and uncle sent to us from New York. I read him a chapter every night, and every night, he fell asleep on my lap. He was always so excited to hear what would happen next, but I wasn't sure if he said that so I would stay with him so he wouldn't be alone in the dark, or if he really did want to know.

That night I lay in bed, trying so hard not to think of all the terrible possibilities that could happen to my family because of the war. They were endless. I tried to fill my mind with medical cures to diseases that no one had found a cure for, but I had nothing. You have to let those kinds of ideas come to you when they do, and not force them.

Sometimes when you think to hard, you get overwhelmed and your brain shuts down.

All the things that happened in the war caused so many overwhelming thoughts and feelings. Some never go away, and us humans have to except that, and just believe that Jehovah God will help us through. At least those were my beliefs, and those beliefs gave me so much faith, and strength. I knew I would be okay, because Jehovah cared for me. He cares for everyone.

I stared at the ceiling, then out the window. The moon was full and bright, and I realized that no matter what happened on Earth, the Sun and Moon would always shine brightly and take turns letting us see their glory. Humans really take advantage of nature, one of the main things that helped me cope.

I thanked God for my beautiful life, and I told him that I would always stick to him no matter what would happen, and I strove to keep the promise, for me and my family.

4

Helma   September 18, 1942

I had a secret. This secret was a secret because my father HATED Jews. I knew this family in our neighborhood that moved to Wisla several months ago, from the Netherlands. The oldest boy, Levi, went to school with me and we got along well. Almost a little too well, for my father's standards. I don't think he ever wanted me to marry, at least until he passed on. He especially didn't want me to be with a Jew. Nazi's were known for their hate towards Jews.

After my ten hour work shift, I scurried to my room to grab my small satchel, then left a note on my bedroom door:

Father, I went to get some groceries, I'll be back in an hour.

I hoped he'd see it, and not punish me for being gone a while.

Walking through thick shrubbery, I arrived in a small cottage area where families settled, but many were feeling unsettled by my father's actions. I sighed and stopped my guilty thoughts about Father.

Walking for about two more minutes on stone paths, and looking at everyone's lovely gardens that were soon to be harvested, I came to a place where Levi and I met every Saturday. We were fine having school days together, but it was nice to have time to ourselves. We were not only a couple, we were best friends too, and I think that's a very important thing to have in a relationship.

I sat down on a stone boulder and looked at the beautiful wild flowers and trees, thick with leaves and moss that created this secret place. I waited about four minutes until I heard,

"Helma?" A familiar voice whispered. It was Levi, stepping around the trees.

I walked over and gave him a hug and a sweet kiss on the cheek. He held his hand on my shoulder and smiled.

"I haven't seen you in awhile," he said as we sat back down on the boulder.

"I know. My father pulled me out of school for a couple days to finish up work in the office." I sighed.

Levi held onto my hands. "Helma, you need to get out of there. Your father is abusive, and the way you talk about the environment at home makes me worry."

"He isn't abusive." I said.

"He makes you hurt inside does he not?" He tucked my golden hair behind my ear.

"I suppose." I looked down at my watch to make sure I'd get back in time to my father.

"Look, you have the standards to have a much greater life than the one you are living. Your father is cruel, and he doesn't deserve being around you," he said.

I smiled, but inside my heart was being tugged. His soulful, brown eyes, gazed into mine, and I this feeling of opia flooded through me.

"I know you want to help, but you don't understand my father. I wouldn't last long out of his authority," I said, hoping he would understand.

"Alright, but I'm going to support you, no matter what," he insisted.

My eyes were watering, but I stopped myself from crying. I gave Levi a long hug, to show that I appreciated him, but nothing would ever be able to completely express that. We talked about how his family was and how it was crazy that soon we would be old enough to make our own decisions, and live a crazy young life. We wanted to live it together.

We said goodbye, and I left the area of cottages. I hurried to the market and bought some carrots and squash that were on sale. I just needed something inexpensive to bring home, since I told my father I was getting groceries. The sun was setting, so I hurried home.

I walked through the back door into the kitchen. Father was opening a bottle of beer. He said it helped him cope with stress, but I disagreed. In my opinion, a nice cup of any kind of tea, is the perfect solution to unbearable stress. I would know.

I put the groceries in the cool box, and put on the kettle.

"Why exactly would carrots and squash be necessary to buy with my money? There is no protein to keep us going," he said without making eye contact with me.

"I thought the vegetables would make a nice side dish to the meat," I said. I could hear my heart thumping. He didn't say anything. He just walked out of the kitchen and downstairs to the office where everyone worked, including me. The office was a basement underground, and our apartment was in the same building, but it was a floor above, and not very big.

I sighed, and went into my bedroom. I sat on my bed and looked at my drawer where I kept all of Mother's old things. I never really had the strength to examine her things. Those feelings of grief never went away, and it was especially hard for me to handle it, since my father no longer felt anything but anger and depression.

Closing my eyes, I took a deep breath. I slowly walked over to the drawer and opened it. It made a horrible squeaking sound that made my nose crinkle up.

I immediately saw a picture of mother and I, when I was about three. She was holding me in her arms and we both had almost identical looking smiles. I could tell Father was taking the picture, because it looked like we were laughing at a joke that he made.

I looked into my mother's eyes. Something I hadn't done for a long time, and it felt strange, and melancholic. I studied her facial features and compared them with mine. I found similarities, but when I looked in the mirror, I looked so much like my father! Why did I have to look like the person I had given up on, who no longer cared or loved me? I looked back down to the photo, and traced my finger along my mother's long, hair. I could still visualize her sitting in front of the mirror, combing her hair, the color of buttermilk. She would run through the locks, getting rid of any knots, then she would carefully pin it away from her face. I would sit patiently on her bed until she finished, then asked her to do the same thing to my hair. A tear rolled down my cheek, and onto my hand. Then another, and another. I missed her so much, and I felt so alone. I wiped my tears and carefully placed the picture where I found it. My eyes moved toward my mother's Bible. I never really took time to learn about the Bible, or trust it, but I still had respect for religious people, unlike my father.

I opened up the cover, and a small paper fell out with a few scriptures written down. I guessed my mother had written down her favorite scriptures that gave her encouragement. The first one on the list was Revelation 21:4. I remember listening to my mother read aloud the Bible to me in the living room. Her voice was soft and modulated. She would read until Father came home from work. When we heard his footsteps walking up to the door, she would quickly hide the Bible under the sofa. I was only about six years old, so I didn't know why she hid it. But when these people came to read the Bible and teach it to her, my father would yell at them to get out.

No matter how mad my father was, Mother still believed that she had found the truth in the Bible, she didn't give up. She would sometimes take me to the people's Church when my father had to work on a

Sunday, and she loved it, but I didn't understand any of the things they talked about. I just went because it made her happy.

Remembering all these things from my childhood, I realized that the Bible changed my mother, and she stayed happy, even when my father became the cruel man he still was. I wanted to feel that too, so I flipped through the very thin pages until I finally found the scripture she had written down. When I read that scripture, my mind was flipped, it made me feel an enormous amount of hope, something that I had only felt a very small amount of in the past ten years. It said: "And God shall wipe away all tears from their eyes; and there shall be no more death, neither sorrow, nor crying, neither shall there be any more pain: for the former things passed away." I was intrigued, I had never read any thing like this before!

I read the next verse, which meant I just had to read the next one, and before I knew it, I finished the chapter. I was shocked.

Every word had brought more and more sense, and happiness to me. I began sobbing with joy in my heart, and I hugged the precious book. If these words were really true, and if my mother had found the truth, I was confident that I could have a better life, just like Levi said.

"Put that evil object down." It was Father. His face was dark and he stared straight at me without blinking. His hands turned into fists, then he moved his wide-eyes to the Bible, grabbed it from my shaking hands, and threw it onto the floor. "Get rid of it." He demanded, and walked out the door.

5

I woke up to the sun shining through the window, onto my face. It felt chilly, but soon the warmth of the early autumn day would absorb last night's rain, and raise the temperature. I liked weather science, figuring out why we have seasons and things like that. Sometimes Klara would call me a science nerd, so I would call her boy obsessed, in return. I guess that's just what good friends do.

I walked downstairs to find Lana and my father at the dining room table, examining some papers and talking. I looked in the kitchen expecting to see Mother, but just saw a plate of toast and eggs on the counter, and a pan in the sink.

Lana noticed me and said, "Oh, that's for you. Mother made it before she left."

"Where is she? And where's Walter and Kacper?" I asked, the house feeling oddly quiet.

"Mother went to the bank, and Walter and Kacper went to the park."

"What?" I said worriedly, "I thought we were supposed to stay safe inside, not go have fun at the park!" I could tell by my father's face, that I was overreacting.

"Calm down sweetheart," Father said, "The park isn't far, and they won't be gone for long. Kacper needed to run around, and Walter kindly offered to take him."

"Plus, there haven't been many incidents in the past day!" Lana cheered. Although, it wasn't as great as she made it seem. I decided they were right, and sat down with my breakfast to listen to what they were talking about.

"The organization allows anyone to contribute food to any friend or family member once a month," Father said. He thought for a moment. "That definitely doesn't include religious literature," He said.

"I'm going to go to the printing department sometime this week, to start making copies of the Watchtowers," Lana said.

"This week?" I questioned. I didn't want her to make the risk so soon in her visit here.

"It says here, that the date we can send in the food is September 20th." She paused. " That's tomorrow!" She exclaimed. Lana quickly got up, grabbed her coat, bag and put on her oxford heels. She opened the door, and Father and I both yelled, "Be careful!"

Father looked at me, sighed, and made a slight grin. I took my last bite of toast, and smiled back.

"Your sister is an ambitious one," he said, "but I've always admired you too Iza. Don't forget that, and don't EVER think that Lana is the favorite child." He got up, and sat next to me.

"I know," I said, my eyes tearing up. I gazed into my father's ocean-blue eyes, and he smiled an encouraging smile. I didn't want my father to get taken away like Klara's.

"Hey, hey, don't cry," he said, wrapping his arms around me and resting his chin on my head. I buried my face in his shoulder. I felt safe.

"I just don't want them to take you. You're the one who keeps our family together," I sobbed.

"Look at me." He held my face in between his hands. "You are strong. I know you can lead our family through whatever happens, okay? You must never give up on yourself, or Jehovah. He's the one who keeps this family together. Everything will be okay." His words felt like cool water on a severe burn. They somewhat healed me, and I felt less weak.

I took a deep breath and smiled. "Thank you," I said, wiping my tears.

After I finished breakfast and cleaned up the kitchen, I sat on the sofa to read a book I was almost done with. Mother came home from the bank, then Walter and Kacper, and eventually Lana. She opened the door and walked in. She was out of breath, like she had run home. I heard Mother say, "Honey! Are you alright? Why are you out of breath?" She said. I looked up from my book expecting to see Lana crying or at least with a worried face, but she was smiling.

"Ten! They gave me ten copies for a great deal!" She exclaimed.

Mother walked into the living room. "Oh that's great Lana! I'm glad you convinced us to work with your idea. Mother said, wiping her hands with a kitchen towel.

"I'm sending in the food and literature tomorrow," Lana explained to Mother.

"Okay, good," She responded while walking back into the kitchen.

"You sure this is going to work?" I said, not to discourage her, but to make sure she realized how risky this was. Although, she is the kind of person who barely gets discouraged anyway.

"I'm sure it is, and if it doesn't, then I'll feel good for trying," She replied.

I smiled and nodded. I trusted her to make the right decisions, and she seemed very confident that the one she was making was the right one.

Lana walked into the dining room to show Father, and discuss more about the plan. I sighed. I was proud of Lana for what she was doing, but I was hoping to spend time with her this week. Just me and her, like we were kids again.

The war changed all of that, and so did time. Lana was older, she had a husband, and new ambitions. I'm sure she didn't want to disappoint me, and she most likely did not realize that she was. She was just so caught up in encouraging the imprisoned brothers, and making Mother, Father, and especially Jehovah proud.

"Iza, can you help me write this word?" Kacper came walking into the living room with a piece of paper in his hand, and a crayon. He placed it down on the small table in the living room, and handed me the crayon. The paper said:

KACPER'S ROOM PLEASE NOCK

I looked at Kacper and I could tell he was thinking really hard while looking at the word NOCK. I smiled. "Is something wrong?" I asked, although I knew what was wrong.

"Yeah, I feel like the last word is wrong, but whenever I sound it out, it sounds right," he said, with a sigh.

"That's because there's a K in the front of the word," I said, looking at him to see the reaction. His eyebrows furrowed, and his lips twisted, created a confused expression

"What? I don't get it." He said.

"I don't really get it either, honestly," I chuckled. "But that's just how it is, sometimes things are just a big mystery that is hard to figure out."

He nodded. "I guess."

I loved these moments, just innocent and cheerful. Finding out new things, forgetting about whatever problems were happening. Kacper helped me feel those moments and he didn't even know. I watched him fit the K into his poster, slow and careful.

Once he finished, he yelled, "Ta-Da!" and put his hands in the air. He ran upstairs to put the sign up, and I walked up and into my bedroom.

I still hadn't got dressed, so I took out a nice dark blue sweater with a peter pan collar, and a black skirt. The sweater was knitted, and perfect for the season. I put them on, and looked in the mirror. I ran my fingers over the embroidered flowers my grandmother made on the collar a year ago. I watered and measured my plants, to find that they were growing nicely.

I took a look at Kacper' sign on his wall; he had splashed some of his favorite colors and drawn a picture of a chameleon below the words. The door was cracked opened. I heard him making plane and car noises and I watched him crash them all together, giggling.

I thought about how his mind must be exploding with imagination, ideas, characters, stories, all the time. That's something I never fully grew out of. I was always imagining fantasy stories, drawing crazy pictures, and laying in bed making up hour long plays in my head that I would just forget later.

I was grateful for my busy mind. I could think of things like that when I needed to stop thinking about bad things, like the war. But with a great imagination, came lots of possibilities that came up in my mind, like bad things that could happen to me or my friends because of the war. Although these thoughts were almost a constant thing, I tried very hard to remember about Jehovah, and all the things my father said to encourage me. I went on with my day, with these thoughts in my head.

September 20, 1942

The next day, Lana was ready to send in the groceries and Watchtowers.

"Honey, are you sure you want to do this? I can send it in instead," Walter said, his voice becoming brittle.

"The brothers need encouragement and I want to give it to them. I can do it, okay?" Lana explained again.

"But you have more family, and more people that care about you," he urged.

"I'll be fine, besides, what's the worst thing that could happen? They won't kill me," she said

"I know."

Lana grabbed her purse and put on her shoes. She looked up at my family and I. She was trying to hide it, but I could see the fear in her eyes. "I'm going alone."

No one responded, and I had given up on stopping her.

Lana put the Watchtowers in the bottom of the bag, and tried her best to make them barely visible. She gave everyone hugs and when she hugged Walter, it looked like they both didn't want to let go, but she did. Walter's eyes were narrowing, preventing tears to drip out. Lana walked out the door and waved goodbye.

I felt drained, and I walked over to the window to watch her walk down the street. Once she went out of my sight, I walked over to the stairs and slowly trekked up them. It was hard to have energy when I had so many worries flooding your mind, and It felt impossible to drain them out.

6

We sat at the small dining room table, awkwardly. My father was eating toast with almond butter and a cup of coffee. We still hadn't talked since two nights ago, when he threw the Bible on the floor. I couldn't stand the awkwardness, so I quickly ate all my food and brought my tea into my room, to get ready for the day. I got dressed, pinned back my long hair, just like how my mother did. I started to get my paperwork together to bring to the office, when there was a quiet knock on my window. I turned around and Levi was standing on the other side of the window, waving. I ran over to the window and opened it up.

"What are you doing here?!" I whispered loudly.

"You want to hang out today?" He whispered back.

I smiled and shook my head slowly. I looked past the window to make sure no one was near us. "My father could have seen you! He might kill you!" I leaned over and gave him a kiss. It was hard to be mad at him. "I'll go tell my dad that I'm going to the library to study for school, meet me behind that tree over there," I said, pointing to a big tree, a couple yards away from our home. He nodded and I closed the window. I grabbed my school bag and slipped on my shoes. I went into the kitchen where my father was still reading the newspaper and drinking coffee. I wondered why he wasn't in the office, working yet.

"Father," I began. He didn't look up. "I am going to walk to the library, I need to use some books for school." I felt no guilt in lying to him.

He just nodded, probably not processing what I had said, and walked out the door. I ran over to the tree where Levi was waiting. There was a small seat in the back of the bike where he put his hand, signaling for me to sit down. I sat and wrapped my arms around his waist. He struggled at first to get the bike pedaling, but soon enough we were on our way out of the residential area of town.

We rode to a small ice cream shop and Levi bought each of us a small cone. He parked his bike, locked it, and we walked to the park. We sat down on a bench and talked for a long time. I complained that I would never get out of my job, and I cried a little too much. He gave me long, warm hugs, and I felt better about talking about it with him. He never seemed annoyed with what I had to say, and he was a good listener.

"Okay, now you've got it all out. Do you feel a little better?" He asked, wiping a tear from my cheek.

I nodded. "Thank you," I said. He smiled and looked at me without a word.

"What?" I asked, laughing.

"I want to show you something," he said excitedly.

"Okay." I replied, eagerly. He got up and opened up the leather bag that was strapped onto the bike. He pulled out a camera, the kind that was popular at the time.

"My uncle sent this to me from back home. Can I take your portrait?" He asked.

My eyes widened. "Sure!" I said delightedly.

"Okay, just stay right where you are," He said, getting the camera ready.

I smiled for the photo and he took it with a huge grin on his face. "That's going to turn out beautiful, Helma," he said, carefully taking the photo out of the camera. "I'll develop it tomorrow after worship. Then, can I keep it?" He asked.

"Of course," I said. He put the camera away and sat back down. I looked at my watch and saw that we had been out for three hours. "I should get home to my father," I sighed.

"Yeah, let's get you home," he agreed.

He rode back slowly, I guessed he didn't want me to leave yet. We arrived at my house and I took a book out of my bag and held it to make it look like I had been studying, in case I saw my father.

"I took you out today because it's all I can do for now," Levi said, looking down.

"What do you mean?" I asked.

"I promised I would help you through what your father does to you, and all I can do is spend time with you and keep you happy."

"And that's all I need from you." I placed my hands on his cheeks and gave him a kiss. I tried to lean back but he pulled me close and gave me a hug. It was long, and comforting, and I rested my face on his shoulder. I pulled back and he put his hat on.

"Thank you Levi," I said. He smiled and tipped his hat. I turned around and headed for my house.

I walked through the back door and into my bedroom. I sat at my desk and took out some homework and books in case my father came in. I didn't actually feel like working on homework, so I walked over to my bed, squatted, and reached for my mother's Bible, which I hid under the bed. I brought it to my desk and opened up to where I had finished. I started reading the first verse when I heard yelling coming from the kitchen.

"Why can't you just investegate it?!" It was my father yelling to one of his workers. "Here take a beer," he said.

"No, I'm okay," the man said.

"Just take it, I need to get rid of some of these before I get too drunk."

There was a heavy sigh. "They found the literature in the grocery bag today," Father began. I was confused, what kind of literature would be a problem? What grocery bag? I kept listening.

"It was a woman around twenty, she was contributing to some Jehovah's Witnesses that we took away from their families." Those words, "Jehovah's Witnesses," sounded familiar, but I couldn't figure out what it was.

"Okay, so what are we going to do about it? How would we find that woman again and arrest her?" The man asked.

"You've been working for me for awhile, and your amount of knowledge makes me want to get rid of you," my father slammed his hand on the table. "I'm sure she put her information down when she sent the bag in, if you can't go figure it out, then I'll just go myself. We can't have these stupid religions smuggling in their publications about the Bible, I just won't allow it," Father said. "Let's go get this over with, let me just go tell my daughter to start an early shift."

I hurried and put the Bible back under my bed, sat at my desk, and pretended to be writing in a notebook.

"I need you to start your shift early," Father was standing in the doorway.

"Okay let me just put away-"

"Just do it! I have to go to the camp to work something out." The camp was the place where my father held undesirables captive. He walked out and I heard the front door open and close.

I wasn't going to stay here working. I needed to find out what cruel thing my father was doing next. I grabbed my bag and went out the front door to follow him. My father didn't have a car. Not many people in the town did; it was so small that there wasn't any use in driving around. It was easy to follow them, and they never looked back so I just walked about ten feet behind.

We arrived at the camp, and Father stepped into the main office where all the guards took breaks and information was stored. I was watching them walk in as I hid behind a bush, and once they closed the door, I sprinted to the back of the building. I spotted a small, open window that was too high up to watch from, so I climbed on top of some crates and boxes and lifted myself up with only the tip of my toes on the box. I peered in to see Father and his worker standing near the door, and a guard, possibly the one who reported the literature, sat in a chair in front of a desk. The desk faced an open window where people sent in things to the prisoners.

"Where is that woman's information that she gave you yesterday?" My father asked, then lowered his voice. "The woman who smuggled the literature."

"Oh yes." The man walked over to a tall file cabinet and opened the first one on the second row. He pulled out a file and took out some papers. He looked through them, put one on the desk, and put the rest of the papers in the file.

"Here is her information," the man handed to my father. Father read it and let his worker take a look as well.

"It shows her home number. Give her a call and tell her to come here, but don't say why," Father said.

"Okay." the man accepted, looking confused. He picked up the phone and dialed several numbers. The room was silent except for the phone dialing. A few moments passed and the man started speaking to someone. "Hello, this is the Gestapo department calling, may I speak to Lana Brook?" He waited a moment. "Hello this is the Gestapo department, you came earlier today and I'd like to speak to you. Please come back here immediately, thank you." He put down the phone. "She'll be here," the man said.

7

It had been a couple of hours since we had sent in the food and literature. Mother was embroidering, Father was outside working in the yard, and Kacper was stacking wood blocks on the coffee table. Lana and Walter were sitting at the table chatting, when the telephone rang. Walter picked it up and listened for a moment. "It's for you," He said, he handed it to Lana.

She listened for about ten seconds, and said, "Yes I'll be there." She put down the phone. "It was the Gestapo, they need me to come back to the prison to talk to me," She said, her voice becoming brittle, "I have to go. The consequences of not going are probably worse than going." She sat down heavily and put her face in her hands.

"I'm coming with you," Walter insisted.

"No, they'll take you away for sure. You're a Brother," Lana said.

"I can hide behind a bush or something," Walter said. " I need to be with you no matter what."

She looked at him and sighed. "Fine, but if I get in trouble, you aren't jumping out and taking a stand for me," Lana laughed.

Walter barely laughed, "Okay."

The back door opened and my father walked in and wiped his forehead with a rag. He obviously felt the tension and quiet in the air because he asked, " What's going on? Is something the matter?"

"Lana just got a call from the Gestapo prison asking for her to come speak to her, most likely about the literature," Mother responded.

Father walked into the kitchen shaking his head. He filled a glass of water and chugged it. He put it down and exhaled, "Who is going with her?"

"Me," Walter said.

I took a deep breath. I had to be there for Lana too.

"I'm coming too," I spoke confidently.

Everyone looked at me. "No honey, you need to stay home with us," Mother said.

"I want to be there," I began. "Lana is my best friend, and if I'm not there for her, I'm not her best friend back." I took another deep breath.

Lana smiled and gave me a hug. "Let's go then!"

We put on our coats and shoes, and I looked behind me to see the rest of my family smiling. They were worried, but proud. I looked at Kacper, and he obviously didn't know what was going on, but he smiled and waved anyway. We walked outside, and the warmth of the sun beamed on my face. I watched Walter wrap his arm around Lana as their footsteps came in sync. I sped up to walk beside Lana. She held the grocery bag in one hand, and my cold hand in the other. We walked into what we knew, could end up in catastrophe.

8

Helma   September 19, 1942

I sat down on the crate and waited for the woman to arrive. I needed to see what they would do to her, so that maybe I could do something about it. About ten minutes passed, and finally, I heard the door open.

"Hello, thank you for coming. We have observed something rather interesting in your contribution to our captives." It was my father speaking now.

I lifted myself up again to peer through the window. There was a woman around twenty three, and a teenager that looked my age, seventeen. They stood next to each other, with the same, confident face.

"And what is that?" The woman asked.

The man showed her some magazines that had been sitting on his desk. I couldn't see well but I squinted my eyes and read the title of the magazine:

THE WATCHTOWER

I recognized it, like I had just seen something like it. Visions of my mother's possessions flooded my mind. I remembered I had seen a magazine just like that in her drawer but I never gave a close look through it.

The woman looked at it and then the floor. "Yes, those were in the bag," she admitted.

Suddenly, there was a noise from the bushes, behind me. I turned my head and saw a man coming from behind the sunblocked forest. His eyes widened and he looked shocked. "I-I- um," He stuttered. He was somewhat tall and had neatly combed brown hair.

"What are you doing here? And who are you?" I asked, trying not to be loud.

"I- uh, came to see my wife," he responded.

I was confused. "There's no one here but me."

"No, she's in there," he pointed at the window.

"That's your wife? The one my father is speaking to?" I asked.

"Yes. Wait, that's your father?"

I sighed. "Yes, that's him, the captain of-" I stopped. "Never mind."

He furrowed his brow. We stood there for a moment.

"Would you like to stand up here to see her?" I asked.

"Sure, thanks." He heaved himself up and looked through the window.

I had so many questions to ask, like, why wasn't he in there with his wife? What is a Watchtower? What was his wife's religion that caused her to so bravely send in the so- called Watchtowers? I didn't ask him, he was so focused on his wife, and watching what was going to happen.

"You know that what you did is against the rules, and I hope you don't expect to be commended for your bravery," my father said.

"No, of course not," the woman said, although, I guessed she was proud of herself anyway.

"And you are going to have to face the consequences," Father said.

I looked over at the man who was standing silently beside me. He looked like he was about to cry, and his hands were shaking.

I noticed that the man that worked there was pressing a button on some sort of device and he talked into it, saying, "Can we get a officer in here? We have a smuggler. It's a woman, age twenty-four."

The woman's eyes were opened wide, like an owl's, and the girl next to her started sobbing. The man next to me had tears rolling down his cheeks, but no sound or movement came from him. He looked shocked. An officer barged in and asked, "Which one?" My father pointed at the older woman.

The officer grabbed her arms and put them behind her back.

"What about this girl here? How was she part of it?" My father asked the woman.

"She didn't do anything, I promise," the woman defended.

"Okay, I'll let it go only once, but if this happens again, it won't be so easy to get by," Father said.

The officer dragged her out of the room, and the girl my age ran out the door.

I looked over at the woman's husband, and he was slowly stepping off the crates. He looked up at me. "What's your name?" He said, wiping his tears.

I was a bit surprised that out of all the things he could say, he asked my name.

"My name is Helma, yours?"

"Walter."

I walked back down and stood next to him. "I'm so sorry, I should have stopped my father, or done something about it."

"No, no, don't feel bad," he said. "There was no way out of it." He looked at me. "You don't like what your father is doing do you?"

"I hate him," I said, and it was true.

"I can't imagine what you have to go through," he said, his voice breaking. I could tell he was trying to get his wife off his mind by asking about my life. "I have to go," he said, and slowly walked around the corner.

I had so many questions I wanted to ask, about the Watchtowers, and he and his wife's religion. My opportunity was lost, and the unanswered questions hung in my head as I walked back home. I wondered if I'd ever see that family again, and if I could find a way to help them.

9

Iza   September 19, 1942

    We arrived at the prison. It was hidden well behind many trees. Walter said he would go find some sort of window he could watch us from, and we went up to the door. Lana gripped my hand and squeezed it tightly. She let go and opened the door. We walked inside to find the man who worked here, and two other men, all standing in the room. "Hello, thank you for coming. We have observed something rather interesting in your contribution to our captives." said one of the men. It was the one with the emotionless, yet creepy, facial expression.

    "And what is that?" Lana asked. She face seemed calm, but her hands were shaking and she took a huge gulp of air. The man who stood next to the desk picked up the Watchtowers that were sitting on his desk. He showed them to us and Lana looked down at the floor. That heavy feeling that you get inside you when you're nervous, felt heavier than I had ever felt before. My hand started to sweat and I felt my face go red.

"Yes, those were in the bag," Lana said admittedly.

"Why is that?" The creepy man asked.

"I am a Jehovah's Witness," she began. "And I needed to give my brothers encouragement because of what terrible things you are doing!" She yelled.

That was a huge risk and I could tell that the men were starting to get mad, but they didn't yell back.

"You know what you did is against the rules, and I hope you don't expect to be commended for your bravery," he said.

"No, of course not," Lana said, but I commended her, and so did my whole family.

"And you are going to have to face the consequences," the creepy man looked even creepier. I realized I had seen him before on my father's newspaper. I thought maybe he was the captain of the many soldiers that came to Wisla and that made me extremely nervous.

I suddenly heard talking from the man who worked here. He was talking into a device, maybe an intercom. "Can we get a officer in here? We have a smuggler. It's a woman, age twenty-four."

I realized at this moment that I could possibly never see my sister again.

My heart was racing, and I felt nauseous. I felt sweat drip off my face, and a couple tears dripped off my chin.

Suddenly an officer barged in and walked straight to me and Lana. " Which one?" He asked.

The captain pointed at Lana.

I watched her face. I could see what she was feeling. It felt like her life was going to be taken away. She would live possibly the rest of her life alone, in a cell, without her family. But she had Jehovah, and I knew that she knew that.

The officer grabbed Lana's wrists and put them behind her back. I briefly held her hand and tried to hold on, but she was pulled away. I looked at her pale, frightful, face one last time. I didn't want to remember her like this, and I hoped and prayed that I would see her again.

"What about this girl here? How was she part of it?" I heard the captain say, and I looked at him to see that he was looking at me, with a stare that goes straight through you.

"She didn't do anything, I promise," Lana said with a short breath in between her words.

"Okay, I'll believe it only once, but if this happens again, it won't be so easy to get by," the captain said, and I felt Jehovah's holy spirit helping me in that moment.

I stared at Lana as she was dragged out of the room.

I couldn't be in that horrid place with those evil men any second longer, so I ran out the door.

I waited on the side of the building for Walter, until I saw him walking around the corner. His eyes were red and there were still some tears resting on his cheeks. He walked slowly, and stared at the ground. Then he looked up at me and I ran over and gave him a long hug. We were both in the same, horrible shocked state of mind.

We walked in silence, down empty, narrow, stone paths and through thick shrubbery, until we arrived home. I took a deep breath as we walked up to the front door. Neither one of us were ready to tell the rest of the family where Lana was, and what had happened.

We walked through the door. Mother and Father were sitting on the couch and Mother had fallen asleep on his shoulder, and it looked like he was just drifting off when Walter and I came in. Father perked up and woke up Mother by tapping her arm. His eyes were wide, and focused on us. Mother woke up and rubbed her eyes. They both realized that Lana wasn't with us and Mother put her hand over her mouth.

Walter sighed, and Father looked down at his lap and held Mother's hand. Mother was still staring at us wide-eyed.

"The Nazis decided that Lana needed to be punished for going against the rules," Walter said. "They arrested her."

Mother's lips were twitching and she sniffled. Her eyes were turning reddish. "How could they?!" She cried. She was sobbing now.

I came and sat next to Mother, and Walter sat in the armchair.

"For how long will they keep her?" Father asked. He was staring at nothing, and didn't look away.

I felt guilt rush through me. "I don't know, I ran out the door before they could tell me," I said. " I'm sorry."

"No sweetheart, it's okay," Mother said, wiping her face with shaky hands.

Now Walter started tearing up, and he got up and walked upstairs. I guessed he needed some time alone, and so did I.

I went upstairs and into my room. I sat down on the floor beside my bed, and wept some more. I thought about how Walter would cope without his love, how Kacper wouldn't fully understand what had happened, and how my parents would deal with practically losing their oldest child. I knew that Mother and Father were in the worst position, but I couldn't help feel that deep, never ending sadness, and uncertainty in my heart. That sadness caused me to ask questions like: Did Jehovah really listen to my prayers? Does he care about us?

Although these questions kept popping up in mind, I still prayed my hardest to Jehovah, and didn't lose faith. I knew that I wasn't the only one in the world who was going through hardships like this, and that God knew how I felt. I thought about our belief that Jehovah will make the world how he originally wanted it to be, perfect, beautiful, and kind. All the dead ones would be resurrected, and no one would ever get sick and die. This hope was in the Bible, and gave me an amount of hope and excitement that nothing else gave me. I knew that I would see Lana again, I just needed to be patient, and so did my whole family. So did the whole world.

10

"You can go to school today, I don't need as much help in the office." It was my father, he was standing in the doorway to my bedroom. His speaking woke me up.

" Oh, okay," I said, sitting up in my bed. I was happy that I could go to school, I needed to catch up on schoolwork and my father and his work had been preventing that lately.

I got dressed and packed my bag, then I quickly ate a hard boiled egg. At about 8:10 am, I left the house. It took about ten minutes to get walk to school, and I arrived when the bell rang. I walked to math class and sat next to my friend, Emily. We weren't that close since we only saw each other in math, but she was kind.

I didn't really spend time with other people besides Levi at school, during break and lunch. And since it was my last year of high school, I didn't feel the need to have a great social life. Besides, my father would probably never let me hang out with a group after school and on the weekends. I just decided to focus on work, college, and reading my mother's Bible. I learned from the Bible a lot, and it helped me keep going.

After math and language arts, I ate an orange and some crackers I had packed, then went to science. Science went by slowly, and so did the rest of the day. I hadn't seen Levi all day, so when the last bell rang, I went to the library to look for him. I knew he went there every Monday to check in and check out books. The library was only a minute away from my classroom. I walked down the small sidewalk towards the front door, but as I walked closer, I heard talking from the small alleyway between the school and the library.

It was a voice that was familiar and heartwarming. A voice that everyday, I looked forward to hear. But why would I hear it right here? Without anyone seeing me, I peered into the alley way, and at that moment, I could feel my heart turning cold, and breaking. All those feelings I had felt in the past four months, disappeared. There it was, the person I had watched laugh and cry, and had loved. But I knew that they didn't love me back the way I thought they did.

"What if Helma sees us here?" It was Levi. His personality that I believed in and appreciated before, was not there. He was a different person.

"It's fine darling." It was a girl, our age. I recognized her from school, but hadn't seen her much. She was beautiful, and had gorgeous, long, black hair.

She held the hands that I had held a million times before, then she kissed the lips that I had kissed with true love in my heart. But I would never again. He kissed her back and tucked a lock of her midnight, black hair behind her ear, just like he did to me. They stopped kissing, but his face stayed close to hers. He smiled and she smiled back.

The anger and disappointment in me pushed the tears out of my eyes. I couldn't let Levi or the girl see me, so I ran all the way home. I ran through the kitchen and upstairs into my room. I lay on my bed and cried into my pillow.

"Are you alright?" I turned my head and saw something I wasn't expecting; my father. I tried to speak, but my words wouldn't come out. I had to force them.

"Yes- um," I wiped my tears and got out of bed.

"Okay, well, I'm going to get some work done in the office," he said.

"Uh, okay," I was surprised, I never thought that my father would ask how I am, or care about my well-being.

He walked out of my room and I heard footsteps down the stairs.

For the next thirty minutes, I looked through some pictures of my mother that I had looked through a million times. I looked at lyrics my mother had written down that she would sing to me, and I was surprised how well I remembered the melodies. I drank lots of tea that afternoon, because it's one out of a few things that helped me get over bad things.

I was singing one of my mother's songs quietly, when I heard a knock at my window. I sighed and looked over. It was Levi, smiling that huge, caring smile. His good looks made it easy for him to fool and cheat people, and I had never seen it like that until then.

I walked over and opened the window.

"I bought some more film, do you want to go take some cool pictures?" He asked.

It was so hard to look away from his deep, soulful eyes, but I did. I reached under my bed to grab a box of all the letters from him and photos that he took of pretty landscapes in his hometown. I held it tightly in my hands, but forced myself to place it in his. My eyes starting tearing up. "You should have these," I said, my eyes not leaving the box.

"Why? I gave these to you to keep," he said.

"I know, and I really loved them." I took a deep breath and closed my eyes. "I thought that what we had, was true.. and I thought that I had made the right decision." I opened my eyes and looked at him. "I thought that I was the one who made you happy.. and-" I blinked and a tear rolled down my cheek. "I- I thought you were real. I trusted you."

His face was bleak and hopeless. He was wiping a few tears with shaky hands. I could tell he was trying to think of what to say, but I didn't let him say anything. "Goodbye." I closed the window and watched him get on his bike. He stared at me for a moment, and it felt like he was tearing my heart open. I stood there woefully, and watched him ride away into the thick forest.

11

September 20, 1942

I walked down the same, old stone path that I walked everyday, coming home from school. That sweet dog was not barking at the neighbor's cat for once, and it walked up to me excitedly, wagging its tail. I smiled and stroked its fluffy, brown fur. It licked my hand and walked away. I kept walking down the path until I arrived home.

"Hi Iza, I'm finding all these cool worms in this dirt pile!" Kacper was squatting in front of the garden, holding a worm in his hand.

"That's super neat Kacper!" I said, walking over to look at what he had found. He smiled.

"Are you going to be a Zoologist?" I asked.

"A what?"

" It's a scientist who studies animals," I explained.

"Yeah, that would be fun!" He said excitedly.

"Take some notes, about what you find, in the journal I gave you," I suggested.

"No, writing takes too long," he complained.

"Draw pictures then," I said, walking into the house.

Father was sitting on the sofa reading the newspaper, and Mother was working on her embroidery. She still had an apron on and I smelled food cooking, so I guessed she was in the middle of making dinner.

"How was school?" My father asked, looking up from his newspaper.

"It was alright," I sighed. I put my school bag next to the door, and sat on the armchair. It almost felt just like before Lana and Walter came, just me, my parents, and Kacper. But there was that loneliness as well. Even though Lana wasn't dead, it felt like she was gone, and that we might never see her again. These feelings were so hard to get rid of, but I kept reminding myself that Jehovah wouldn't let the world stay like this forever, and that he cared for me, and would let us see Lana again.

"Oh no!" It was my mother coming from the kitchen.

"What is it?" My father asked, getting up from the sofa.

"I didn't realize the recipe has six cups of flour. I don't have enough and I already started cooking," my mother said frustratedly. "Iza, can you take a quick stop at the market and get me some more flour? I sent Walter to get some things, but I didn't ask him for flour."

I sighed. "Sure. I'll keep a lookout for Walter so we can walk home together."

"Alright, thank you sweetheart," she said.
I grabbed my school bag and took out the books and papers, and left my money, sketchbook, and pencils in the bag. Then I left the house.

After walking back on the lovely stone trail, I arrived at the market. It wasn't as busy as I thought it was going to be, since most people shop for groceries at this time of day. I stopped by the stand that sold bread, pastries, and flour.

"How much is a five pound bag of flour?" I asked the man working there.

"That's one zloty," he said, without modulation. He must have said that so many times.

I handed him the money and he handed over the flour.

"Thank you very much," I said, trying to lighten his mood.

"You're welcome. Have a nice day," He said with a droning voice.

I walked through the other stands just to see if there was anything new. I realized I wouldn't be able to carry much more with the big bag of flour in my hand.

"Hey Iza!" It was a voice I had heard before. I turned around and saw a young brother my age that had just moved into our congregation. We had only talked a couple times before, but he seemed like a nice person.

"Oh hi Noah!" I said.

"How are you and your family holding up with all this stuff happening?" He asked.

I got a vision of Lana being dragged out of that room, and the captain smiling contently. I shuttered. "Um, its been ok. Well, not really. Lana, my sister, got arrested for trying to send in Watchtowers to the brothers in prison," I said, trying not to cry again.

"Oh, I'm so sorry, I shouldn't have asked about it," He apologized.

"No, its okay."

"You know, if you and your family don't feel safe at your house, you can always come and stay with my family since we live more in the countryside, out of town,"

"That's very kind. I'll let my parents know." I smiled.

"Do you need help carrying that bag of flour?" Noah asked.

"Oh um, sure. I was wanting to buy some of that jam, but I didn't have enough hands," I said, and handed him the bag.

We walked over to the jam stand, and I bought blackberry and raspberry jam.

We walked through the stands, and I spotted Walter, holding a basket of groceries, heading towards the end of the market.

"Oh, that's my brother-in-law who I'm meeting up with," I said to Noah, pointing at Walter. "Let's go catch up with him."

We sped walked over to Walter and I tapped him on the shoulder. He turned around. "Oh hi Iza, who's this?" He asked.

"This is Noah. He's a new brother in our congregation who moved in with his family from Debica." I explained.

"Oh yes, I recognize you from worship," Walter said. "Nice to meet you."

"You too," Noah said.

"Well, Walter, we should be getting home," I said.

"Oh, here's your bag of flour," Noah said, handing one to me and one to Walter.

"Thank you," I said.

As Walter and I walked home, I tried to lighten his dreary mood by telling funny stories about Kacper when he was a baby, like how he called me his brother, no matter how many times I said, "No Kacper, I'm your sister!"

Walter laughed with me and we arrived home with smiles on our faces, but as we walked closer to the house, I saw two men. The same men that were there when Lana was arrested. One, the captain, had that same, evil look on his face. Next to him was the soldier who stood next to him on that day that Lana was taken, and the other was the soldier who dragged her away.

I was worried and shocked. My hands started sweating and I felt hot.

I watched the captain yell at my father. As he stood silently in front of the men, my father looked fearless and strong.

My mother came running out of the house and grabbed Kacper. She pulled him over to the front door, and they watched from a distance.

"You! Your daughter has broken the rules! So have all of you! You and your disgusting God!" The captain thundered. "I can't stand all this!" He shouted, baring his teeth.

Kacper started whimpering, and Mother was sobbing while one hand was on her mouth and one was holding Kacper tight.

The Captain pushed my father to the ground, but he got back up.

"Take him," The captain yelled to his soldiers. "Take him!!"

"No!" My mother cried out.

I ran to my mother and Walter followed. I felt my body weaken, because the foundation of our family was getting taken away.

I watched helplessly as the soldier grabbed my father's arms and pulled them behind his back, just like he did to Lana.

"Looks like your stupid god, Jehovah, isn't helping you now, is he?!" The Captain yelled at us.

The soldier was pulling my father further and further away each second, and I felt my heart pulling towards him.

"No! Kacper! Come back!!" My mother screamed.

I looked over and saw that Kacper was sprinting fast towards my father and screaming. "Father!! Come back!" He flung out his arms to attack the other soldier, tears falling to the ground. The soldier saw him and hit Kacper's chest with the butt of his rifle and Kacper flung to the ground, hitting his head on a large stone. He started shrieking with pain.

Mother, Walter and I all ran to Kacper. My knees fell to the ground and I put my hand on Kacpers head.

"Kacper! You're going to be okay!"
He started gasping for air as blood kept pouring uncontrollably out of his head.

"I'm- scared," he croaked,"I'm-scared."

"I know, I know," Mother said. She grabbed Kacpers hands and kissed them.

Kacper's breathing kept getting heavier, and faster, and he tried to speak, but just cried. "I can't see you! Where are you? It's blurry!" He yelped.

"I'm right here buddy! I'm not leaving you!" I sobbed. My heart was racing and I felt nauseous. I felt sweat and tears drip off my face, and I allowed this overwhelming feeling take over my body. Tears wouldn't stop raining from my eyes, and I tried to wipe them away, but it felt as if they would never stop. I could tell he could barely breathe anymore, and I put my hand on his heart and it felt like it was beating out of his chest.

Then it stopped. It was silent. He stopped gasping.

Mother was still holding Kacper's cold hands, and Walter had been stroking his head, but now was just resting his hand there. I looked up and the soldiers were gone. Father was gone. Kacper was gone.

12

Helma   September 21, 1942

I organized the many piles of paperwork on my desk. My father ended up needed help in the office that day, and it was hard to concentrate on the work.

"Sir, I found the address you asked for," I heard a man say in a fake, gruff voice. It was that same man who was yelling at the young soldier a few days ago and who was there when the woman got arrested.

"Okay. I'll go there now, I just need to get this over with," My father replied to him. He grabbed the paper and walked over to me. "Can you write this down?"

I took out a blank piece of paper.

"7996 Bukowa road," he read off the paper. "Now we'll have an extra copy just in case," he said to the man.

I wondered why he was going to this place, and I decided to go there too since I had just written the address down. Maybe I could actually defend the poor people my father attacked and treated unfairly.

I waited about 10 minutes so that I wouldn't be right behind them, then I quickly put on my coat, and slipped out the door. I hoped no one in the office saw me.

I followed the stone path I would walk to meet Levi, and I hoped I wouldn't see him, I just kept walking, keeping my focus on where I needed to go.

I arrived at 7996 Bukowa road, it was a medium sized home, with a beautiful garden in the front. I hid behind the trees and bushes. I spotted my father.

He was standing in front of a little boy lying on the ground, with three people sitting around him. I couldn't tell if the boy was dead or not, and if he was, I strongly hoped it wasn't my father's fault.

But when I looked at my father, tall and wide-eyed, I didn't see even a spark of love, or humanity. He was gone, not physically, but inside, he was dead. It seemed as if he had forgotten the past. His beautiful wife, and daughter that he had loved, were just another worthless trophy on his shelf.

The family wept over the boy, I couldn't imagine how it must feel to lose your own child. I only knew what it was like to lose a mother, and if that was heartbreaking, then losing something you created and grew, must truly be just as devastating. I could tell that my father was about to leave, so I went on my way. I tried not to weep, as I quickly walked back to the office. I was so mad at my father and I just couldn't handle watching him do all these things anymore.

"Helma!" I turned around and immediately regretted following my father, for he had caught up with me. My heartbeat accelerated and I tried to take short breaths to calm myself.

"Why aren't you at the office?" He asked, anger building up, showing it in his face.

"I-" I began.

"You better tell the truth!"

I took another deep breath and closed my eyes. I had to stand up for myself. But when I opened my eyes again, fear came raining down again as I stared into my father's pupils. For the first time in my life, I prayed. I prayed to God in my head, asking for help because I had put up with this for so long, I knew I deserved strength.

"Father," I began. "You can't keep doing this, I miss the old you, the real you! And even though you don't want it, I know that you can have love and happiness in your life! I know with no doubt that this job doesn't make you happy, and I've found something that can make you happy, something that makes me happy and made Mother happy!"

He stared at me unbelievably, and a tear streamed down his face.

I hoped that the words that I had been keeping locked inside me touched his heart, and he could be who he was again. He took a step closer to me, and I panicked. I thought maybe he would hit me, or yell back, but as he got closer, he wrapped his arms around me, into a hug. As he held me in his arms, I felt the realness of God, and the things I had read in the Bible were true. It was like God had switched something in my father's head that made him really look at himself.

Bang!

I heard my father gasp, and collapse to the ground. I looked up and didn't see anyone. I pulled myself to the ground to see where my father had been shot. I spotted blood leaking out of his leg. I was obviously not happy that it was his leg, but I was definitely relieved that it wasn't his heart, or neck. I ran as fast as I could to the closest house, and banged on the door.

13

September 21, 1942

My mother sat on the sofa, her eyes wide, rarely blinking. She had no tears left in her, as she stitched up her second embroidery piece. Embroidery usually helped her cope, and get her mind of things, but I knew that it wasn't helping a bit.

Walter had called the local morticians, and they had just arrived to pick Kacper up. How could someone have that job? It's a daily procedure for them to take a soulless human, and bury them under the Earth. I guessed you have to be very emotionally strong to do that.

I couldn't bear to watch Kacper get driven away. I just stared at the floor, with a blanket wrapped around me, and a cup of tea in my hand. My throat hurt from crying, so I kept sipping the tea to soothe it.

The front door opened, and Walter walked in. "We need to get out of here, maybe to the country. It's just not safe here in town," he said.

"I suppose," Mother replied, still looking down at her work.

"The country," I said, then I remembered about what Noah had said to me. " Mother, do you remember the Mroczka's?

"Yes, they just moved into our congregation recently," she said.

"I know, and I saw the oldest boy, Noah, at the market today. He said that his family would always welcome us to come to their home in the country, which is less than a mile away from here," I explained.

"That would be smart to stay there," Walter said.

Mother sighed. "I don't want to make such a hard decision right now."

"It's not a hard decision, if we choose to go stay with them, we'd possibly be choosing to stay alive!" I insisted.

"Let's pray about it," Walter suggested.

"Good idea," I said, and Mother nodded.

Walter said the prayer, while my mother and I listened, closing our eyes. After, I felt a little better, and I was reminded about God's promise of a resurrection of the dead, and that nothing like this would happen when

Jehovah made the Earth perfect again. I was grateful for the family that was still here with me, and that I wasn't alone.

"We can't give up, okay? We can't give up on Jehovah," Walter urged.

I felt so bad for Walter. He just got married to Lana, came here willingly to be with her family, and he couldn't be with her anymore. He was probably so distressed, and missed her as much as my family did, but he was good at not showing those feelings. Now he was trying his hardest to help my mother and I.

"You're right Walter, we should go. Helena gave me their address a couple weeks ago, in case of something like this. Let's leave tomorrow morning," my mother decided, being more confident.

I was surprised how my mother's mood changed so quickly, and it motivated me to be more determined too.

"Okay," Walter said, and then I said the same.

Walter took off his shoes and went upstairs.

"Iza, darling," my mother began. "Come here."

I sat up, walked over to the sofa, and sat next to my mother, resting my head on her shoulder. She put aside her embroidery, and held out her hands, facing the ceiling, on my lap. I lay my hands on hers, held them, and she held mine back. We looked up at each other, her pupils were big, and shimmering. "I am so proud of you, Iza," she said, "You've been so brave, and I love you very much for that." She paused. "We aren't giving up, just like Walter said." Her voice was soothing, like a beautiful melody.

"Thank you, I love you too," I said. With Father in prison, we were going to need lots of comfort and strength from each other.

She wrapped her arms around me, and held me like I was still a small child. Every second, I felt more calm, and every second, I buried more and more sadness away, trying to focus on the ones who were still around me.

As I watched the soft rain tap on my bedroom window, I drifted into sleep, with Kacper locked into my heart, forever.

14

September 21, 1942

"Someone please help!! My father has been shot!" I screamed, and started to sob. I noticed there was a 1935 Austin Ten car parked in their driveway, that maybe these people would drive my father to the hospital.

The door swung open and a young, African, man was standing there. "What is wrong?" He asked. I guessed he was from Africa or someplace like that, because he had a very heavy accent. A woman quickly walked over to us with a worried look. She looked Polish.

"My father was just-" I was out of breath. "Shot in the leg! Can you take him to the hospital with your car?"

The man widened his eyes. "Yes, of course. Where is he?"

I pointed towards my father, who was lying on the other side of the road. The man and possibly his wife, sped out the door and we ran across the street.

The man looked at my father and realized who he was. I could tell he was scared.

"Help me pick him up. Be careful of the wound," he said, and we both leaned over to pick my father up awkwardly.

"Go bring the car over here," The man said to his wife.

The car drove over to the other side of the road. We opened the passenger seat door and carefully placed my father in there. He was moaning, and gripping the side of the seat. I gently closed the door, and got in the back seat. The wife sat in the seat beside me. We started driving, and I watched at all the houses we past.

"What's your name?" She asked me. She had a beautiful French accent.

"Helma. What's yours?" I asked, wiping my face that was wet of tears.

"Camille, and this is my husband, Kojo."

"Nice to meet you," I said, looking at my lap. I didn't have great social skills, so it was hard to make eye contact

"You are strong." I felt her squeeze my hand.

I looked at her, she was smiling brightly.

It was hard to remember the last time I had been treated so kindly before. Besides Levi, but I tried not to think about him. She had such a kind face, and light brown eyes, that turned golden in the sunlight. I still heard my father moaning in pain, and I prayed for him to be okay.

We arrived at the hospital in about four minutes, and we parked right in the front. Kojo jogged into the building and I could see him talking to a doctor. The doctor seemed considerate, and urgent to help the patient. They walked outside and the doctor said something to two men, then kept walking towards the car. He quickly stepped around the car to where my father was sitting in the passenger's seat.

"Alright," he took a look at the wound.

Two men came, around the car as well, pushing a stretcher. They carefully picked up my father and lay him on the stretcher, with the doctors help.

"We'll take him to the emergency room and then get him a room. Please follow," the doctor said.

Kojo, Camille and I all got out of the car and followed the doctor. One of the men was pushing the stretcher in front of us.

We walked into a small, bright room, that had an unpleasant smell that made me a little nauseous.

A young man that looked like an assistant or apprentice was sitting at a desk. He stood. He looked up and was staring at my father.

"What can I do to help, Doctor?" He asked, his nervous face toughening up.

"Help me clean the wound and I'll get some surgeons to remove the bullet," The doctor replied. He turned to my father. "Keep taking deep breaths sir."

Camille put her hand on my shoulder. "Come on, let's go in the waiting area."
I turned around, nodded, and followed her out the door. Kojo was sitting on one of the chairs placed beside the room my father was in. Camille sat next to him, and I sat in the chair next to her.

"Thank you so much for helping my father, I really admire you for it," I said to them.

They both looked at me and smiled.

"You're welcome, we are happy to help," Camille replied. Kojo was nodding as she spoke.

We sat quietly for a few moments, and then I said, "I'm so sorry."

They turned their heads, and looked concerned.

"For what?" Kojo asked.

"My father," I looked down. " He has done so many evil things that I just watch and don't do anything, at least in the moment."

"Don't you dare be sorry, Helma," Camille said sternly. "You are so brave to help your father, even though you've seen him do those actions."

I looked at her, and grinned. I tried to keep my eyes from watering. Even though I hadn't known them for even a day, they felt like family. Like I had known them my whole life.

"Before he got shot, I told him how I felt. About how he needed to look at himself, and that I needed a real father." I explained. "He hugged me, and it felt like I had been holding my breath forever, and I could finally take a fresh breath of air."

Kojo's smile was almost the biggest, happiest smile I had seen. "You are very brave Helma. You did the right thing. Maybe your father will reflect on himself," he said.

I nodded.

"Thank you for waiting so patiently." The doctor walked outside the room. He was holding a clipboard and a pen. "What is your relationship to the patient?" He asked the three of us.

"My name is Helma. I'm his daughter, and these are my friends that helped my father get here," I said.

He wrote something down on his paper, probably my name. "Fortunately, we took out the bullet successfully, and stitched the wound. The injury is in his calf, and so it's a good thing he didn't get shot in a joint. He will have to be on a cast for about six months or so, and it will take about eight or nine months until he can walk normally again."

It was a lot of information to take in all at once. This was so sudden. First, the words I had been holding on to for so long, exploded in my father's face, he showed appreciation for what I said, and then he was hurt.

I wasn't surprised someone had shot him, almost the whole town was furious at him, and for some reason, I felt responsible. But Camille and Kojo helped me remember that I was strong.

I looked at the doctor's name tag, which said, "Dr. Tyminski."

"Thank you for treating him so quickly Doctor Tyminski," I said.

He smiled. "It's what we do here, and I'm happy to help. Is there someone you'd like me to call, to let them know about the situation?" He asked, probably wondering about a mother, or family member.

I thought about my father's workers. Those were the only people that were closest to family. But still not family at all. I didn't want to call them.

"No, it's alright. Thank you," I responded.

Dr. Tyminski nodded. "Your father will be here for some time. You can stay here if you'd like, but it is your choice," he said to Camille, Kojo, and I.

I could stay home alone. I was used to it.

"I'll go back home, and come back to see him tomorrow," I said.

"We'll go back home," Kojo said, then turned towards me. "And Helma, you are always welcome to our home, if you don't want to be home alone," he offered. Camille nodded in agreement.

"Thank you so much, I'll just stay at home for now," I said.

The doctor went back into the room.

Camille took out a small notebook and pen from her purse and wrote something down. She ripped out the paper and handed it to me. "This is our home phone number, just give us a call if you need anything at all, okay?"

"Thank you," I said again.

"Do you need us to drive you home?" Kojo asked.

"No, I'm going to sit with my father for a little bit. My house is closer if you go the opposite direction of yours, anyway," I answered.

"Okay," Camille said. She gave me a hug, and so did Kojo.

I watched them walk outside the building, then I poked my head through the door where the doctor was working at his desk. His assistant was cleaning the tools in the sink. I turned my head from the sink because I didn't want to see the filthy tools.

"Excuse me," I said, not wanting to interrupt their work.

They both noticed me. Dr. Tyminski shifted his upper body towards me, ready to listen, while the assistant only glanced up at me, and continued his work.

"May I see my father?" I asked, stepping into the room.

"Yes, of course," the doctor responded, putting down his pen. He looked over at his assistant. "Come on, let's let her have some time alone with her father."

"Oh, um, I'm not done yet," the assistant said shakily.

"You can finish cleaning later." The doctor patted his shoulder, and motioned him to follow. I took a deep breath, slowly walking over to my father and sitting in the chair next to the bed.

15

September 22, 1942

I swung a sack full of some of my clothes and books of mine, over my shoulder. We didn't know how long we would stay at the Mroczka's home. It felt like we were evacuating from a natural disaster, like a hurricane, or tsunami. But we were escaping from people, and that was very disappointing. I felt my confidence in most humanity lowering.

We cut through the stone path, and headed into the fields. It was a bit marshy out in the grass, from the constant rain every night. But getting our shoes a little muddy was the least of our worries.

After about thirty to forty minutes, we came to the Mroczka's house. It was a small, welcoming, stone farmhouse. There was a chimney that sat on the top, right of the house, and smoke was slowly drifting out of it, soaring into the sky. The vegetable and flower garden spread around the house, and looked well taken care of.

We walked up to the front door, and wiped our feet on the mat that lay beside the big, carved, wooden door. The air was chilly, and it smelled of burning wood and fresh rain.

Walter knocked on the door, and a moment later, the youngest child, Marie, opened the door. She was about four, and just tall enough to reach the doorknob.

"Hello!" She said excitedly, realizing she knew us.

The mother, Helena, came jogging over to Marie. "Honey! Why did you answer the door? You know that either me or Papa answers the door," she said sternly.

"I'm sorry," Marie apologized. Her big eyes were looking up at her mother.

"Hello! It's good to see my fellow brother and sisters!" Helena said joyfully to us, and she gave us all hugs. "Come in."

We stepped inside and I smelled a newly cooked breakfast. A medium sized dog ran up to us, wagging his tail. I pet his fluffy, white fur, and scratched behind his ear.

"Hello," Noah greeted us, as he walked into the room, from a hallway.

"Hello," we responded scatteredly.

"I'm so glad you all are here now, further away from danger, and being with our fellow brothers and sisters, brings us closer to Jehovah, doesn't it?" Helena asked.

"Yes it does," my mother replied.

I watched Helena's eyes, and they were looking as she had realized something.
"I heard about Lana, but where is Kacper and your husband?" Helena asked.

There was a moment of silence as we thought about who should say the news.
"My husband was taken away by the Nazi's, and they-" my mother blinked, and a tear dribbled down her face. "They killed Kacper."
Noah and Helena's white of their eyes widened, and their faces darkened.

"I'm so sorry," they took turns saying.

"Thank you," Mother said.

There was another moment of silence, then Helena said, "Noah, can you show them where they can settle?"

Noah nodded, and walked into the hallway while we followed. He showed us the room, and we placed our bags on the full sized bed, and twin sized.

We all headed into the kitchen, where Helena and Marie were both setting the table for breakfast. Noah started putting the food on the table, and I helped, while Walter and Mother sat at the table.

We ate a delicious polish meal, consisting of warm bread rolls, gorące płatki owsiane, hard-boiled eggs, and hot tea. Helena talked about the move from Debica, and how difficult it was, but also how they could see how much Jehovah helped them through it. We had more boring talk about how school was for Noah and I, and Walter illustrated his hometown in England.

I wasn't much of a contribution to the conversations, but when I did say something, they all listened, and nodded their heads with understanding. It made my feel appreciated, and not just an extra in everyone else's play.

I was so relieved, that not once did Helena ask about how we were holding up with Father and Lana gone, and losing Kacper. I did not want to start crying again, and I was sure Mother and Walter didn't want to either.

After breakfast, we cleaned up and all went out in the garden to do yard work, trying to distract us from the thoughts that hung in all of our minds. Noah and I chased their dog, Aussie, and got so tired that we collapsed on the grass. Aussie started licking our faces, and we laughed so hard, I could barely catch a breath. It was nice to have a few moments, almost forgetting that it could be the last joyful moment that I'd have.

The dog lay next to me, and I turned my head to Noah, who was already smiling at me.

I smiled back, gazing into his gleaming, hazel eyes. Aussie got up and started licking my face again, trying to get us up. We started laughing again, and got up from the dewy grass.

The rest of the day was just spent relaxing, getting to know the Mroczka's more, and reading helpful scriptures together to stay faithful in Jehovah.

When I lay in bed that night, the image of Kacper, gasping for air popped in my head every other minute, until I finally drifted off. I was broken, but the care from this family, and the care from Jehovah, comforted me, and I felt as if I was being binded back together.

16

He was lying there, breathing steadily. It was strange to see him so calm, not yelling at his soldiers, or the poor people he hated just because of what they believed. In that moment, I could imagine my father being the father I'd always wanted. One that would listen to what I did that day, who would have long conversations at the dinner table with me, and who would comfort me when I needed it.

The only reason I needed comforting at the time, was because of him. He was the one that caused me pain all my life, and the only person I had that would comfort me, was Levi. But that was over, and I was so glad that I had spoke up to my father, and maybe once he would wake up, things would be a little better.

I sat there, taking in everything that had happened in only the past few days. It was overwhelming, and I wanted everything to be over. I wanted the War to be over. All those people my father took away from their families, to come home, that small child to be alive and well, my mother to be here, holding me tightly. Most of all, my father to wake up already, and I could hug him. I was so nervous that my father wouldn't go back to when I told him how I felt, and he would just go back to being dull, and cruel. Was I overthinking it all?

"Helma.." my father croaked.

I looked up, tears filling my eyes, but I held them back.

He smiled proudly, and held out his hand. I stared at it nervously, pulled my hand closer to his, and held it.

"Thank you Helma." A tear dropped off his face, but he was still smiling. He pulled my hand up to his face, and kissed it weakly. "I'm so sorry. I have been a terrible man. I was blinded."

"I know," I said, but I still couldn't forgive him. We needed time to reconnect. My nose was clogging up from crying, and it felt like my eyes were swollen. I let go of his hand, and wiped my nose with my handkerchief. "Since you can't right now, I'm going to try to help the families you hurt," I said, with confidence.

He looked ashamed, but still smiled weakly

"You should get more rest, Father." I said, lifting myself up from the chair.

He nodded.

I walked over to the door, opened it, and looked back at him.

"I love you Helma," he said nervously. He hadn't said that in years.

I wanted to say it back, but my words wouldn't come out of my mouth. Did I really love him back? I smiled, stepped out of the room, and closed the door behind me.

The walk back home was long, and quiet. I went into the apartment, and into my bedroom. I immediately lay in bed with my dress still on, and fell asleep.

In the morning, I ate breakfast, then when into the office and started walking towards the area where most of the other desks were. "My father has been shot in the leg," I announced.

They all glared up at me at once, like clones, and it made me shiver.

"Why did we not know this?" one of the workers blurted out.

"When did this happen?" another asked.

"Just yesterday. I sent him into the hospital, and he is doing well," I answered, and they went back to work.

I walked across the office to get to my desk, and I heard quiet crying. It was coming from the dining area where the soldiers ate their meals. I peered into the crack of the door, and saw the young soldier who had I remembered gotten yelled at by my father's worker, a couple days ago. He was putting his face in his hands, and crying. I decided, I needed to help him out, so I opened the door wider and walked in.

"Are you alright?" I asked him.

He quickly looked up and started drying his tears. "Er, yes, I'm okay, I just am struggling with my job at the moment. I never chose to do this, and I hate hurting people." He had very light, almost blond hair, and grey-blue eyes.

I sat down across from him. "I can understand." I reached from my pocket and took out the small paper with the family's address written down. "What do you say we get out of here?"

He perked up.

"I need your help, I need you to act like you are going to the hospital to see my father who is the boss. He got injured yesterday," I explained.

"And what would we really be doing?" He asked.

"I have this family I need to help. I can take them to a safe place. My father killed their son, and took away two of their family members, because of their religion."

"Okay." He grinned. "I'll go."

I told him my name, and he told me his: Peter.

We snuck out of the office, and headed towards Bukowa road, which is where the house was. We walked down those same old stone paths, and passed Levi's home. When we got to the house, no one was outside, so we walked up to the door, and knocked. No answer. We knocked again. No answer. I looked into the window, and it was dark inside. I sat down on the steps in the front yard.

"Well, they aren't here, I guess we'll just go-"

"Helma, there's soldiers over there." Peter said.

I looked up, and saw four soldiers, walking towards the countryside. I got up, ran closer to the soldiers, and hid on the side of the house, so I could listen.

"We'll see if they will sign the pledge, and if they don't, then we take them to jail. Good?" One of the soldiers spoke.

"What if they're talking about the family?" I whispered to Peter.

He shrugged.

"Let's follow them, maybe we can help the family escape," I murmured.

And we did, and I was proud. I was going to do what my father didn't. I wanted to help.

17

Iza   September 23, 1942

I walked down the hallway and into the kitchen.

"Good morning!" Noah said happily, as he was making breakfast.

"Good morning," I replied. I felt refreshed, and the smell of hot tea and eggs filled my nose.

"Did you sleep well, Iza?" Helena asked me. She was sitting in the living room with her husband Harold, my mother, and Walter. They all had mugs in their hands.

"Yes, thank you again for the hospitality," I replied. I had been a little too cold the night before, but I didn't want to mention that. It was still raining outside, but the furnace was glowing, giving us warmth.

"Do you need any help with breakfast?" I asked Noah.

"Sure, you could mix this a little more," he handed me a big bowl with a mixture in it. I didn't know what it was, but I just did what he told me to do.

A young couple from our congregation came to stay after we made breakfast. They lived in the middle of town as well, and also needed to get out into the country.

The morning was long and delightful; we had a hearty breakfast, and visited. The pain that was caused by Kacper's death was till so present in us, but we stayed occupied.

There was a loud knock at the door.

We were silent. The steam from our food was the only movement, until Helena just slightly opened the blinds, and looked outside. Her face became fearful. She turned to us. "Noah. Get them in the attic."

Everyone was glancing at each other, with eyes full of fear, and confusion. Noah motioned for everyone to head to the attic.

"Noah," Helena said.

He looked at her.

"Once you close the attic door, do not open it," she commanded.

He nodded, and me, Walter, Mother, and the young couple, who were Kojo and Camille, followed Noah to the attic.

Noah pulled down the ladder, his hands shaking. Everyone was shaking. We quickly climbed up the ladder, and crawled into the very tight space attic. I sat close to Mother, and she squeezed my hand.

I looked around at all of us, and for some reason, I felt something missing. What was missing?

"Noah, your sister!" Mother whispered loudly.

The door was shut.

Tears fell down Noah's face, my face, and everyone's faces. Noah slowly crawled next to me and sat down. I put out my hand for him, and he held it tight. The raindrops were battering on the roof, and the harder it rained, the tighter Noah squeezed my hand.

No one spoke, we just listened to the Nazi's stomping into the home below us.
The words were faint, but loud enough to hear.

"Sign these papers to renounce your loyalty towards your religion," A soldier boomed. "Or we will send you to prison."

I looked at Noah. His eyes were fearful, red, and full of tears. Watching him be so scared about possibly never seeing his parents again, made tears fall out of my eyes as well.

What good could happen now? Every part of my life was getting taken away, one by one. I felt hopeless. Did everyone?

I looked at the young couple, Kojo and Camille. Camille was gripping Kojo's arm, and he was holding her head as she leaned it on is shoulder. He gave her a kiss on the forehead.

I turned my head to my mother and Walter. Walter was clenching his jaw and closing his eyes. I could tell he was trying to stay calm, but this moment had nothing settling. Mother was wiping the tears caused by trauma, fear, and sadness. She had always been brave, and she still was, at this moment.

Then I looked at Noah. He had a gentle heart. He was such a kind, and happy person, and to see him in such emotional pain, gave me pain. His parents could either leave him forever, or destroy their belief in the most valuable thing in the universe, Jehovah God.

Noah was gripping my hand. It hurt a little bit, but I was never going to let go until he did.

We sat there. In the attic. I was strong, but the strength was draining out of me, just like the leak in the roof would drip endlessly.

The window of the attic opened. A blonde girl was putting her head through it.

She had a smile of excitement, but eyes of fear. But you can't be brave without being afraid. I looked at Mother, she was confused. Noah's tears stopped, and his grip on my hand was loosened. Walter was smiling, and so were Kojo and Camille.

Then the girl spoke, with a courageous German accent, "Come on, we'll get you out of here! We're here to help."

Epilogue

Iza

Those years that the war took place in, affected me for the rest of my life, but I tried my hardest to fill my life with joyful things.

After that young German girl, Helma, and her friend, Peter, helped us escape the attic, we all fled to Czechia. The trek was long, and exhausting, but eventually, we arrived in a very small town, called Nydek, Czechia. We met up with the congregation of Jehovah's Witnesses in that town, and they showed hospitality to us so kindly.

We were constantly moving, fleeing from persecution that I almost got used to. We took a train to Germany, and when we got there in early October, we received word that my Father had been sent to work in a mine with one other brother because they refused to join the military. Even though my father was doing extremely difficult labor, my family was relieved he had a fellow brother to work alongside him. We sent letters to him, and we didn't know if they ever got to him, because he never sent any back.

Thankfully, we were in Germany for only three weeks, then took multiple train rides to the Camille's hometown in the coast of France, where we settled for about six months. I finished up my last year of school, and we saved money to get to America. A month before we left France, Walter decided to go back to his family in England. He said he needed to wait for Lana, and to support his parents and siblings. It was hard letting him go, he had been such a vivid part of my family.

Finally, we got seven tickets for me, Mother, Noah, Kojo, Camille, Helma, and Peter, for a huge passenger ship, to New York, U.S.A. I was so excited to be in America, and to feel more safe.

We all started finding places to live, creating new friendships, and getting jobs. Lana was eventually released and traveled back to England to reunite with Walter. She immediately wanted to see my mother and I, so they came to New York for a few weeks to stay with us.

Once I moved out to stay with Helma in her apartment, Noah and I started dating. We dated for about a year, and then got married in 1947. Two years later, Noah, Peter,

Helma, and I all went to Gilead, a bible based school to train to become missionaries, located in upstate New York. Once we graduated, Noah and I were sent to Thailand to support the congregations and teach others about the bible. I fell in love with Thailand, and it felt like the place I was meant to be.

Helma and Peter were sent to Zambia. It was hard to be so far away from our best friends, but nothing made us happier than doing things for Jehovah after all the things he had done for us. Helma and I are still the best of friends, and we keep in touch all the time, despite being thousands of miles apart. She is one of the strongest people I know and I will always admire her. If it wasn't for her, I might have died while still in Poland.

World War II brought so much pain and suffering to the whole world, and many Jehovah's Witnesses were killed during it. Yes, it is the most difficult trial I've faced, but if I didn't experience it, I wouldn't be as faithful, strong, and grateful then I am now. I would possibly not have married the kindest man I know, since we bonded through our pain, and I wouldn't have met my best friend, Helma. I wouldn't have made so many amazing friendships all around the world, and work as hard to accomplish my goals. I don't ever complain about the war, but I view it as something that I learned so much from, and has made me a better person. I am now 27 years old, and I am awaiting a new little person into my life. I hope to share this story with them and they can learn from it, that Jehovah does care about everyone of us and will help us out of every bad situation, if we obey him and are faithful.

Epilogue

Helma

Since the day I found my mother's bible, I have had a whole different mindset. I've made better decisions, I have been so much more courageous and kind.

When Peter and I arrived at Iza's home, we found no one there, so I went to the office and took another address that my father had planned on raiding. So once we arrived at this home which was the Mroczka's, I helped them all escape from the attic. Iza and I immediately became friends, and her and her family showed how grateful they were towards me. I don't take all the credit for helping her and her family and escaping Poland, for Jehovah God is truly the one who led us out of our misery.

We traveled across Europe, finding our way crossing the Atlantic Ocean, to America. Through our time traveling, I became so very close to the Sadoski's (Iza's family) ,Kojo, Camille, and especially Peter. Him and I studied the bible with a local sister, and got baptized on the same day. We could relate to each other the most, and I found him to be a very positive and loving man, despite being a former Nazi soldier. We dated for for about a year and a half, then married in 1948. We rented out a good sized apartment in central New York near Iza and Noah's home, and Peter got a job in a repair shop. In the span of two years, we worked our way to being regular pioneers for preaching the good news of the bible. We were calmly settled, when we got invited to the school of Gilead. I was very happy to be starting a new chapter of my life, and I knew it would be a good one.

We graduated Gilead, and got sent to Zambia, Africa, to support the preaching and teaching work. I had lived in three countries: Germany, Poland, and America, and they were all pretty different from each other, but Zambia felt like a whole other world. It was difficult, but also fun to explore a new culture and befriend people so different from Europe and America, and it felt amazing to take such a big leap for Jehovah.

Because I was so far away from Iza, we would send letters to each other as often as we could. We chatted over letters just as we would being together in real life. Iza and I are still kindred spirits, and she is the most kind-hearted, and supportive person I know.

After my father was fully healed, he sent his soldiers and workers back to Germany.

He too wanted to leave Wisla, so he came to New York to be with me and my new family. He started studying the bible, and found his love for reading. Because of loving to read, and the need for a job, he opened a book shop, and everytime I saw him he was a more calm, and loving man.

In 1942, when we lived in Wisla, I would have never imagined him to become the man he is today. He is baptized, and a regular pioneer.

The war changed so many things, but to see where it got me, makes me happy that I lived through it. It made me courageous, and faithful in Jehovah.

Made in the USA
Middletown, DE
13 January 2021

31484464R00064